# All About Bears

Songs and stories about bears
who live all over the world.

Story by:
Ken Forsse

Illustrated by:
David High
Russell Hicks
Rennie Rau
Theresa Mazurek

**WORLDS OF WONDER™**

Grubby™  Newton Gimmick™  Princess Aruzia™  Leota™  Wooly What's-It™  Prince Arin™  Fobs™

Page 1

A Koala's nose is soft.
A Koala's nose is round.

A Koala knows exactly
who would like him
hanging 'round.

Have you ever thought about a Panda?

The Arctic is really a strange place to be but Polar Bears still live there.

They went to a place with palm trees and sand.

There are lots of Bears.
Brown bears, and Black
bears, and Grizzly bears,
and Himalayan bears.

Teddy Bear, the kind of friend who'll follow you just anywhere.

Teddy Bear, somehow none of your other toys can quite compare.

O.K. Teddy, my confusion
is pretty much cleared up.

My best friend is an Illiop.

HARD TO
FIND CITY

MOSS
FOREST

KING
NOGBURTS

WIZARD OF WEE GEE

GRUNG

TREMBLY
FAULT

MUSHROOM FOREST

THE GREAT DESERT

Land of
GRUNDO